SUDLERSVILLE ELEMENTARY SCHOOL

How Night
Came from the Sea

A Story from Brazil

Retold by MARY-JOAN GERSON   Pictures by CARLA GOLEMBE

Little, Brown and Company
Boston New York Toronto London

To Charles, with whom I've taken some of life's most wonderful journeys.
And special thanks to Ann Rider of Little, Brown for her enthusiasm and support.
M.G.

For Julie Leavitt, Beth Damsky, Paula Goldstein, and Linda Schiller,
who also dance to tropical rhythms. Thank you to all the spirit voices.
C.G.

This tale was recorded early in this century by Elsie Spicer Eells in her book
entitled *Fairy Tales from Brazil: How and Why Tales from Brazilian Folklore*
(New York: Dodd, Mead, 1917). For the telling in this book, the male sea serpent
was transformed into Iemanjá since in the Candomblé and Yoruba religions,
she is the goddess of the rivers and seas, one of the important goddesses
in the Yoruba pantheon.

Text copyright © 1994 by Mary-Joan Gerson
Illustrations copyright © 1994 by Carla Golembe

All rights reserved. No part of this book may be reproduced in any form or
by any electronic or mechanical means, including information storage and
retrieval systems, without permission in writing from the publisher, except
by a reviewer who may quote brief passages in a review.

First Edition

Library of Congress Cataloging-in-Publication Data
Gerson, Mary-Joan.
    How night came from the sea : a story from Brazil / retold by Mary-Joan Gerson ;
pictures by Carla Golembe. — 1st ed.
        p.   cm.
    Summary: An African sea goddess brings the gift of night to the land of daylight,
thus permitting rest for the workers under Brazil's hot sun.
    ISBN 0-316-30855-2
    [1. Fairy tales. 2. Brazil — Fiction. 3. Night — Fiction.]
I. Golembe, Carla, ill. II. Title.
PZ8.G337Ho 1994
[E] — dc20   93-20054

10 9 8 7 6 5 4 3 2 1

NIL
Published simultaneously in Canada by Little, Brown & Company (Canada) Limited
and in Great Britain by Little, Brown and Company (UK) Limited

Printed in Italy

The pictures in this book are monotypes, or one-of-a-kind prints. The process is a
combination of painting and printmaking. A painting is made using oil-based inks on
a piece of Plexiglas. Then while the painting is still wet, it is transferred to a paper
by means of an etching press. After the print is dry, it is often worked into again
with oil pastels, colored pencils, or gouache.

Author's Note

From the seventeenth through the nineteenth century, millions of Africans were captured and shipped to work as slaves in the New World. Of the ten to twelve million sent to all of the Americas, the country of Brazil in South America received the greatest share — between four and five million. They were brought over to work the huge tobacco and sugarcane fields and the rich gold and diamond mines. Today Brazil remains the country in the Americas with the largest number of people of African descent.

Faith crossed the ocean, too, and thrives today in a religion called Candomblé (kahn-dome-BLEH), which is a complicated blend of African beliefs. Candomblé is an important religion in the Northeast of Brazil, in a region called Bahia (bah-EE-ah). This Bahian story tells about a goddess of that religion. Her name is Iemanjá (ee-eh-mahn-JAH); she is goddess of the sea, and she was first worshiped as Yemoja by the Yorubas of West Africa. Since Brazil is a country half-lined by seacoast, Brazilians often pay tribute to Iemanjá for her many gifts. Once a year Brazilians worship the sea goddess by floating offerings of flowers at the edge of the ocean; they hope that the flowers will not sink but float out to sea as a sign that she accepts them. Through their devotion to Iemanjá, Brazilians express gratitude for the richness of what the ocean yields to them, as well as their awareness of an unbroken connection to Africa and its ancient heritage.

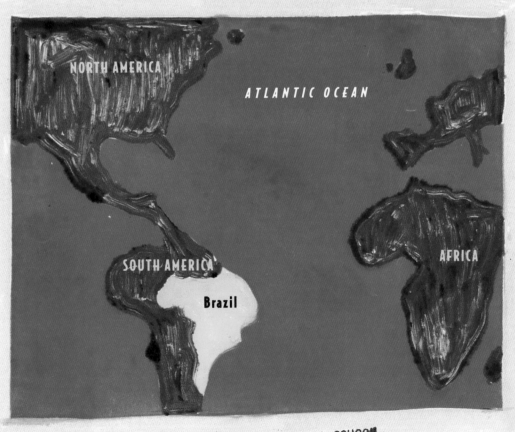

SUDLERSVILLE ELEMENTARY SCHOOL

Long, long ago, at the very beginning of time, when the world had just been made, there was no night. It was always daytime.

No one had ever heard of sunrise or sunset, starlight or moonbeams.
There were no night creatures such as owls and tigers, and no night
flowers that secretly open their petals at dusk. There was no soft
night air, heavy with perfume. Sunlight always filled the sky. The
light jumped from the coconuts at the top of the palm trees and it
gleamed from the backs of the alligators wading at the edge of the
sea. Everywhere there was only sunlight and brightness and heat.

In that time, the great African goddess Iemanjá dwelt in the depths of the sea. And Iemanjá had a daughter who decided to marry one of the sons of the earth people. With sorrow and with longing, the daughter left her home in the deep ocean and came to live with her husband in the land of daylight.

Iemanjá's daughter loved her husband, and she loved the magic of daylight that he showed her: the shimmering sand of the beach, the rows and rows of cocoa and sugarcane baking in sunlight, and the sparkling jewels and feathered costumes worn in harvest festivals.

But with time, the light became too bright and hard for Iemanjá's daughter. The sight of the workers bent over in the fields day after day hurt her eyes and her heart.

And finally even the brilliant colors worn by the dancers at the festivals burned through her drooping lids.

"Oh, how I wish night would come," she cried. "Here there is always daylight, but in my mother's kingdom there are cool shadows and dark, quiet corners."

Her husband listened to her with great sorrow, for he loved her. "What is this night?" he asked her. "Tell me about it, and perhaps I can find a little of it for you."

"Night," she said, "is like the quiet after crying or the end of the storm. It is a dark, cool blanket that covers everything. If only we could have a little of the darkness of my mother's kingdom to rest our eyes some of the time."

Her husband called at once his three most faithful servants. "I am sending you on a very important journey," he told them. "You are to go to the kingdom of Iemanjá, who dwells in the depths of the seas. You must beg her to give you some of the darkness of night so that my wife will stop longing to return to her mother's kingdom and will be able to find happiness on land with me."

The three servants set forth. After a long, dangerous journey through the surging waves of the ocean, over the cliffs of underwater sand, and past the razor-sharp reefs of coral, they arrived at the palace of Iemanjá. Throwing themselves at the feet of the goddess, they begged her for some night to carry back with them. "Stand up, you foolish men," she commanded. "How can you beg a mother whose child is suffering?" And without a second lost, she packed a big bag of night for them to carry through the circling currents of water. "But," she said, "you must not open this until you reach my daughter, because only she can calm the night spirits I have packed inside."

SOULERSVILLE ELEMENTARY SCHOOL

The three servants pulled the big bag alongside them as they swam back through the cool, swirling sea. Finally they emerged into the bright sunlight of the shore and followed the path home, bearing the big bag upon their heads. Soon they heard strange sounds. They were the voices of all the night creatures squeezed inside. The servants had never heard this strange chorus of night screeching before, and they shook with fear.

The first servant stared at the screaming bag of voices and began to tremble.

"Let us drop this bag of night and run away as fast as we can," said the second servant.

"Coward!" said the third, trying to sound brave. "I am going to open the bag and see what makes all those terrible sounds."

He laid the bag on the ground and opened its sealing wax with his teeth. Out rushed the night beasts, the night birds, and all the night insects. Out jumped the stars and the moon. The servants ran terrified into the jungle.

But the servants were in luck, because Iemanjá's daughter was standing at the shore, waiting and waiting for their return. Ever since they had set out on their journey, she had stood in one spot under a palm tree at the edge of the sea, shading her eyes with her hand and praying for the darkness. And she was still standing in that spot when the servants let night escape.

"Night has come. Night has come at last," she cried as she saw the blue-black shadows gather on the horizon. "I greet you, my kinship spirits." And when she spoke, the night spirits were suddenly calmed, and there was hushed darkness everywhere.

Then the gentle hum of the night creatures began, and moonbeams flickered across the sky. The creatures of the night appeared before her: the owl hunting by moonlight and the tiger finding its way through the forest by smelling the dark, damp earth. The soft air grew heavy with the smell of night perfume. To Iemanjá's daughter, this

coming of night was indeed like the quiet after crying or the end of the storm. It was like a dark, cool blanket covering everything, and just as if a soft hand had soothed her tired eyes, Iemanjá's daughter fell fast asleep.

She awoke feeling as if she were about to sing. How rested she was after the coolness of her night dreams! Her eyes opened wide to the brightness of the glistening day, and in her heart she knew she would find peace in her husband's land. And so to celebrate the beauty of her new home, Iemanjá's daughter made three gifts.

To the last bright star still shining above the palm tree she said, "Glittering star, from now on you will be our sign that night is passing. You shall be called the morning star, and you will announce the birth of each day."

To the rooster standing by her, she said, "You shall be the watchman of the night. From this day on, your voice will warn us that the light is coming."

And to the birds all about her she called, "You singing birds, you shall sing your sweetest songs at this hour to announce the dawn of each day."

To this day, the gifts of Iemanjá's daughter help celebrate each new sunrise. In Brazil the early morning is called the *madrugada*. As the *madrugada* slides onto the horizon, the morning star reigns in the sky

as queen of the dawn. The rooster announces the day's approach to
the sleeping birds, and then they sing their most beautiful songs.

And it is also true that in Brazil night leaps out quickly like a bullfrog just as it leapt quickly out of the bag in the beginning of time. The night flowers suddenly open their petals at dusk. And as they do, the owl and tiger begin their hunt for food.

The beasts and birds and insects of the night begin to sing their gentle chorus. And when the dark, cool blanket of night covers everything, the people of the earth take their rest.